THANKFUL

For Mom and Dad
Whatever tomorrow brings,
I love you
—E. V.

For you
—S. C.

SIMON & SCHUSTER BOOKS FOR YOUNG READERS
An imprint of Simon & Schuster Children's Publishing Division
1230 Avenue of the Americas, New York, New York 10020
Text © 2021 by Elaine Vickers • Illustrations © 2021 by Samantha Cotterill
All rights reserved, including the right of reproduction in whole or in part in any form.
SIMON & SCHUSTER BOOKS FOR YOUNG READERS is a trademark of Simon & Schuster, Inc.
For information about special discounts for bulk purchases, please contact
Simon & Schuster Special Sales at 1-866-506-1949 or business@simonandschuster.com.
The Simon & Schuster Speakers Bureau can bring authors to your live event.
For more information or to book an event, contact the Simon & Schuster Speakers Bureau
at 1-866-248-3049 or visit our website at www.simonspeakers.com.
Book design by Lizzy Bromley • The text for this book was set in Pencil Pete.
The illustrations for this book are hand-built three-dimensional
sets photographed with a digital SLR camera.
Manufactured in China • 0621 SCP • First Edition
2 4 6 8 10 9 7 5 3 1
Library of Congress Cataloging-in-Publication Data
Names: Vickers, Elaine, author. | Cotterill, Samantha, illustrator.
Title: Thankful / written by Elaine Vickers ; illustrated by Samantha Cotterill.
Description: First edition. | New York : Simon & Schuster Books for Young Readers, 2021.
| "A Paula Wiseman Book." | Audience: Ages 4–8. | Audience: Grades K–1. | Summary: When
the first snow falls, a girl writes on strips of paper what she is thankful for, from a safe and warm
home to wishes come true, as her family makes a thankful chain.
Identifiers: LCCN 2020056790 (print) | LCCN 2020056791 (eBook) | ISBN 9781534477346 (hardcover)
| ISBN 9781534477353 (eBook) • Subjects: CYAC: Gratitude—Fiction.
Classification: LCC PZ7.1.V533 Th 2021 (print) | LCC PZ7.1.V533 (eBook) | DDC [E]—dc23
LC record available at https://lccn.loc.gov/2020056790
LC eBook record available at https://lccn.loc.gov/2020056791

THANKFUL

Words by Elaine Vickers
Pictures by Samantha Cotterill

A Paula Wiseman Book
Simon & Schuster Books for Young Readers
New York   London   Toronto   Sydney   New Delhi

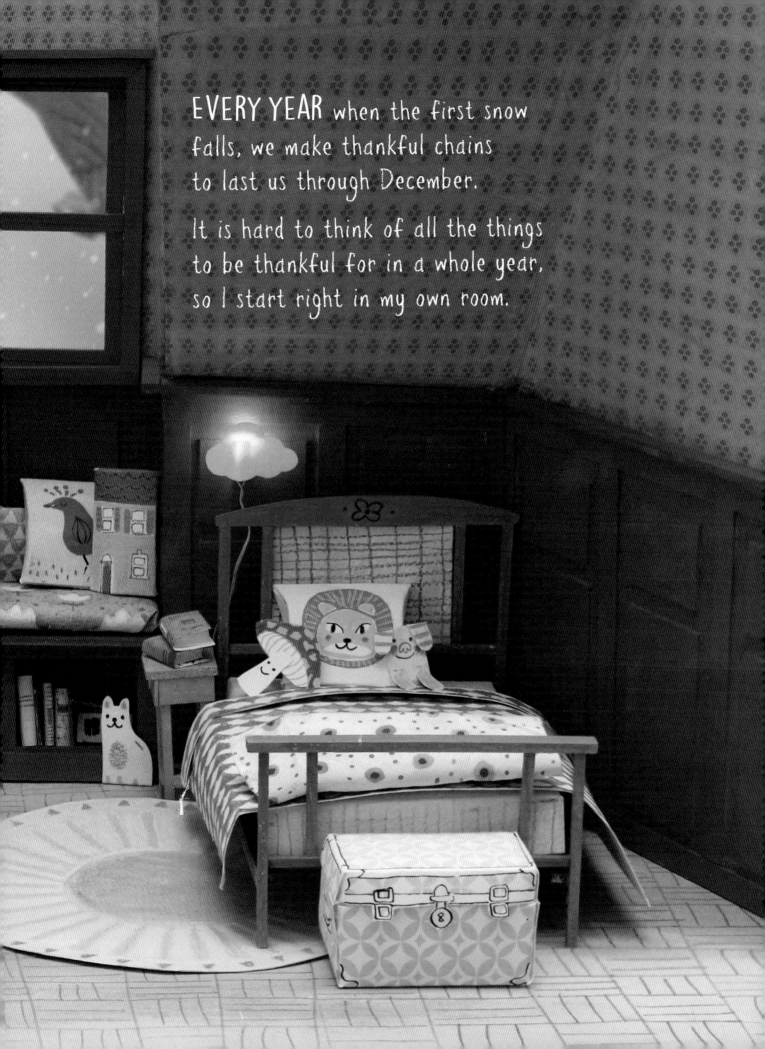

EVERY YEAR when the first snow falls, we make thankful chains to last us through December.

It is hard to think of all the things to be thankful for in a whole year, so I start right in my own room.

I am thankful for a home
where I am safe and warm.

Thankful for parents who
read me stories and brush
my hair gently, gently.

Who whisper the same
poem every night when
they tuck me in.

"Good night, dream sweet things,
let them carry you on their wings,
and whatever tomorrow brings,
I love you."

I am thankful for all those things:

love and dreams,

night and morning.

For a moon and a sun
that always come back.

For stars and candles
to make my wishes on.

I am thankful for my wish that came true:

a dog, round and soft, that wiggles
and jumps when I am happy

and comforts me when I am scared.

I am thankful for a heart that beats,

tuc-tuc,

tuc-tuc,

and every breath,

in and out,

in and out.

I am thankful for
a friend who waits
for me at recess

and a teacher who knows
when I am trying my best.

I am thankful for
doors that lead to
wonderful places

and books that do that too.

I am thankful for
things that are warm:

soup

and socks

and the spot under
the covers where someone
has just been sleeping.

I am thankful for . . .

things that are cold:

icy water in my
favorite cup,

a cloth on my forehead
when I feel sick,

snow that softens
the whole world.

I am thankful for
things that are soft
and fresh, like
laundry,
bread,
moss on rocks.

For things that are hard,

like pedals and

handlebars and

a smooth road for riding bikes with friends.

And I am thankful for . . .

stop signs and seat belts and
things that keep me safe.

Scraped knees and ripped jeans
and things that get fixed.

For wind

and sand—

but not at the same time.

I am thankful for COLOR.

And pencils and paper to tell my stories.

My ideas keep connecting,
one to another to another,
until I am too sleepy to
think anymore.

"Come," my parents say.
"Let's get you to bed."

As I pull the quilt to my chin,
my parents say those special words,

"Good night, dream sweet things,
let them carry you on their wings,
and whatever tomorrow brings,
I love you."

Tomorrow, my family will read aloud the first links in our thankful chains.

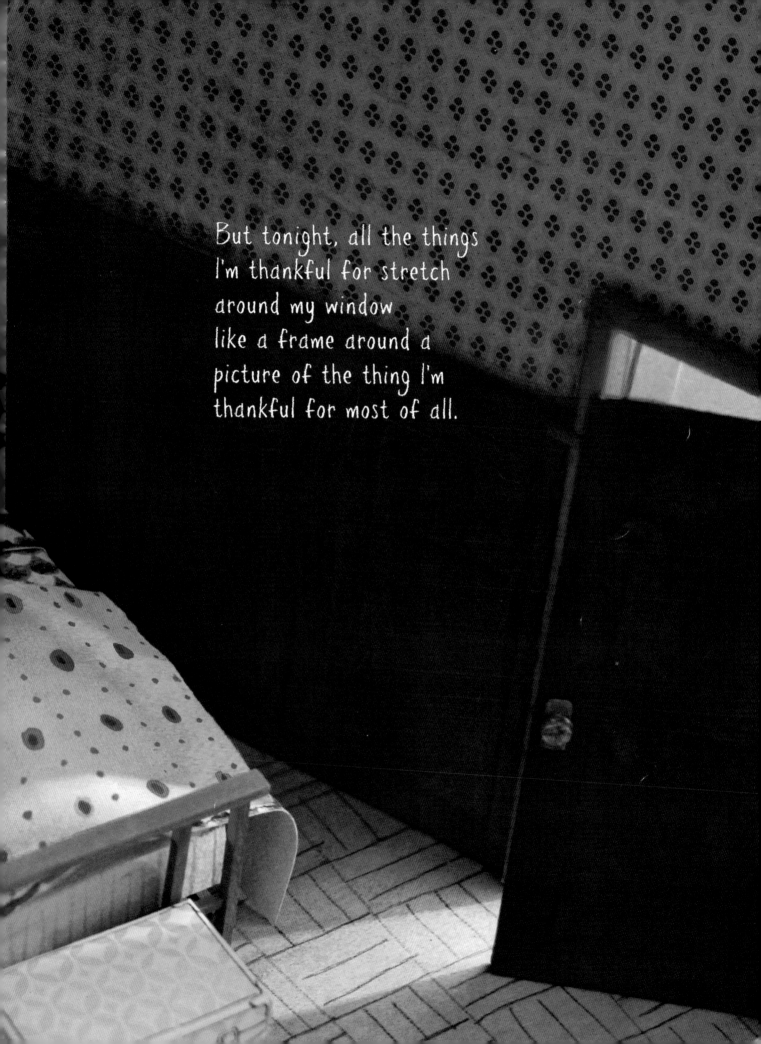

But tonight, all the things
I'm thankful for stretch
around my window
like a frame around a
picture of the thing I'm
thankful for most of all.